P9-EEU-371

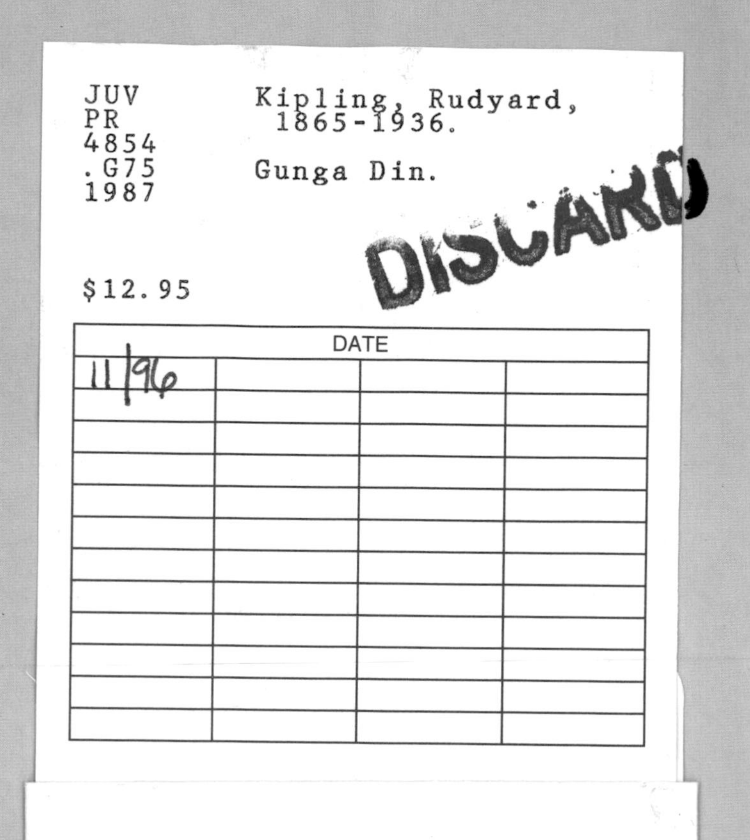
JUV
PR
4854
.G75
1987
Kipling, Rudyard,
1865-1936.
Gunga Din.
DISCARD
$12.95
DATE
11/96

Rudyard Kipling was uniquely equipped to portray life in India under the British Empire in all its abundant variety. He was born there, in Bombay, and was brought up largely by native servants. From the age of seventeen he was a newspaper reporter, travelling all over the subcontinent and talking with people of every nation, culture, religion, and status. Among these were the ordinary enlisted men of the British army, whom he came to know and to understand as no one else ever did. He sympathised with their lot and warmed to them, too, coarse and ignorant though they generally were, awkward to handle like soldiers anywhere but capable of loyalty, unselfishness, compassion, and even respect for individuals of other races—not very common a hundred years ago.

Kipling celebrated the qualities of the British soldier in his *Barrack-Room Ballads*, first published in 1890 when their author was still only twenty-four years old, in style and subject matter an achievement unparalleled in English. They were soon wildly popular, not only in print but also as recited and sung in the Victorian music halls and at smoking concerts. Among them, "Gunga Din" was always a favourite, and some of its phrases, notably the last line, are still current today. The story is based on a then-famous incident of the ferocious Indian Mutiny of 1857, and Gunga Din himself was modelled on a heroic water-carrier at the siege of Delhi in that year.

—Kingsley Amis

GUNGA

GULLIVER BOOKS
HARCOURT BRACE JOVANOVICH
San Diego Austin Orlando

DIN

by Rudyard Kipling
Illustrated by Robert Andrew Parker
With an introduction by Kingsley Amis

FOR MAX BENKERT

December 7, 1960
October 23, 1984

HBJ

Requests for permission to make copies of any part of the work should be mailed to:
Permissions, Harcourt Brace Jovanovich, Publishers,
Orlando, Florida 32887.

Library of Congress Cataloging-in-Publication Data
Kipling, Rudyard, 1865-1936.
Gunga Din.
"Gulliver books."
Summary: An illustrated edition of the classic poem, in which a British soldier recalls his experiences in the army in India and pays homage to the courage of the Indian water carrier Gunga Din.
1. India—Juvenile poetry. 2. British—India—Juvenile poetry. 3. Children's poetry, English.
[1. India—Poetry. 2. British—India—Poetry.
3. English poetry] I. Parker, Robert Andrew, ill. II. Title.
PR4854.G75 1987 821'.8 86-19388
ISBN 0-15-200456-4

Printed in Hong Kong
First edition
A B C D E

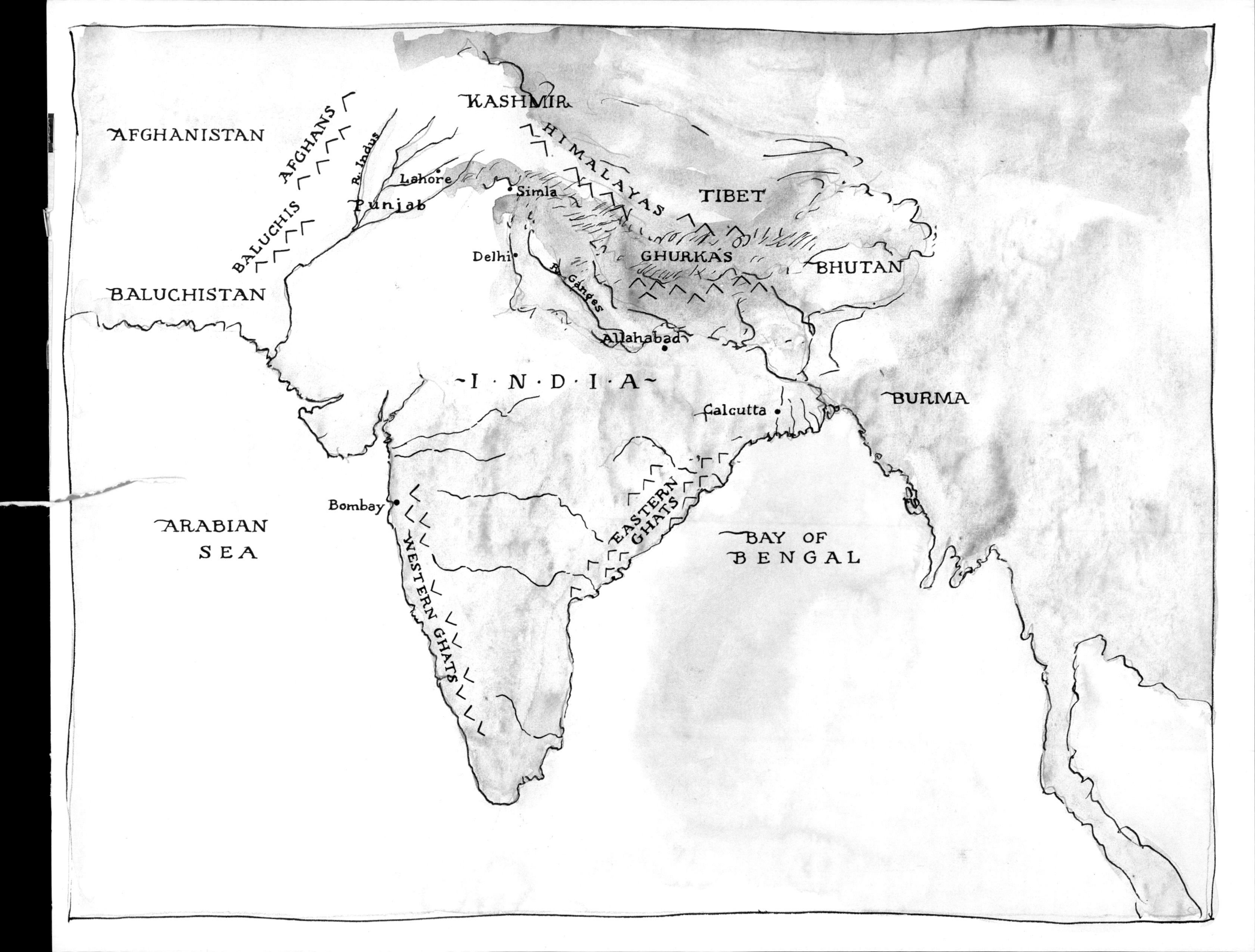
KASHMIR
AFGHANISTAN
AFGHANS
R. Indus
Lahore
Simla
HIMALAYAS
TIBET
Punjab
BALUCHIS
Delhi
R. Ganges
GHURKAS
BHUTAN
BALUCHISTAN
Allahabad
I · N · D · I · A
BURMA
Calcutta
EASTERN GHATS
Bombay
ARABIAN SEA
BAY OF BENGAL
WESTERN GHATS

You may talk o' gin and beer
When you're quartered safe out 'ere,
An' you're sent to penny-fights an' Aldershot it;
But when it comes to slaughter
You will do your work on water,
An' you'll lick the bloomin' boots of 'im that's got it.

Now in Injia's sunny clime,
Where I used to spend my time
A-servin of 'Er Majesty the Queen,
Of all them blackfaced crew
The finest man I knew
Was our regimental *bhisti*, Gunga Din.

bhisti: water carrier

He was "Din! Din! Din!"
"You limpin' lump o' brick-dust, Gunga Din!
"Hi! slippy hitherao!
"Water, get it! *Panee lao!*
"You squidgy-nosed old idol, Gunga Din."

Panee lao!: Bring water swiftly!

The uniform 'e wore
Was nothin' much before,
An' rather less than 'arf o' that be'ind,
For a piece o' twisty rag
An' a goatskin water-bag
Was all the field-equipment 'e could find.

When the sweatin' troop-train lay
In a sidin' through the day,
Where the 'eat would make your bloomin' eyebrows crawl,
We shouted *"Harry By!"*
Till our throats were bricky-dry,
Then we wopped 'im 'cause 'e couldn't serve us all.

Harry By!: O Brother!

It was "Din! Din! Din!
"You 'eathen, where the mischief 'ave you been?
"You put some *juldee* in it,
"Or I'll *marrow* you this minute
"If you don't fill up my helmet, Gunga Din!"

juldee: quickness
marrow: hit

'E would dot an' carry one
Till the longest day was done,
An' 'e didn't seem to know the use o' fear.
If we charged or broke or cut,
You could bet your bloomin' nut,
'E'd be waitin' fifty paces right flank rear.
With 'is *mussick* on 'is back,
'E would skip with our attack,
An' watch us till the bugles made "Retire."
An' for all 'is dirty 'ide
'E was white, clear white, inside
When 'e went to tend the wounded under fire!

mussick: water-skin

It was "Din! Din! Din!"
With the bullets kickin' dust-spots on the green.
When the cartridges ran out,
You could hear the front-files shout,
"Hi! ammunition-mules an' Gunga Din!"

I sha'n't forgit the night
When I dropped be'ind the fight
With a bullet where my belt-plate should 'a' been.
I was chokin' mad with thirst,
An' the man that spied me first
Was our good old grinnin', gruntin' Gunga Din.
'E lifted up my 'ead,
An' he plugged me where I bled,
An' 'e guv me 'arf-a-pint o' water-green:
It was crawlin' and it stunk,
But of all the drinks I've drunk,
I'm gratefullest to one from Gunga Din.

It was Din! Din! Din!
" 'Ere's a beggar with a bullet through 'is spleen;
" 'E's chawin' up the ground,
"An 'e's kickin' all around:
"For Gawd's sake git the water, Gunga Din!"

’E carried me away
To where a *dooli* lay,
An’ a bullet come an’ drilled the beggar clean.
’E put me safe inside,
An’ just before ’e died,
“I ’ope you liked your drink,” sez Gunga Din.

dooli: litter

So I'll meet 'im later on
In the place where 'e is gone—
Where it's always double drill and no canteen;
'E'll be squattin' on the coals
Givin' drink to poor damned souls,
An' I'll get a swig in hell from Gunga Din!

Din! Din! Din!
You Lazarushian-leather Gunga Din!
Tho' I've belted you and flayed you,
By the livin' Gawd that made you,
You're a better man than I am, Gunga Din!

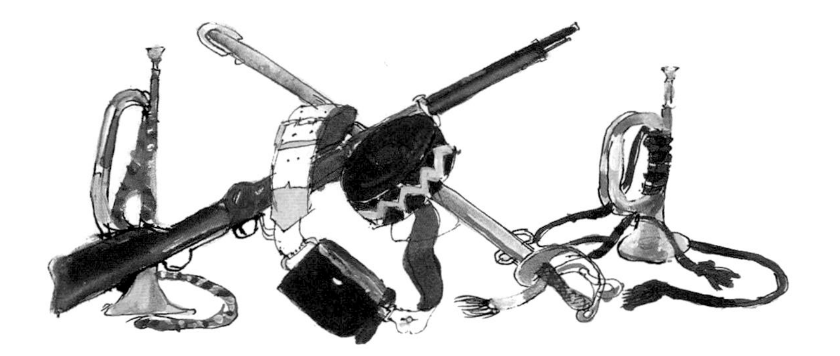

The illustrations in this book were done in watercolor with some gouache.
Text type was set in Palatino by Central Graphics, San Diego, California.
Display type was set in Augustea by Thompson Type, San Diego, California.
Printed and bound by South China Printing Company, Quarry Bay, Hong Kong
Production supervision by Warren Wallerstein and Eileen McGlone
Designed by Dalia Hartman